The Schernoff Discoveries

Gary Paulsen

A YEARLING BOOK

Published by
Bantam Doubleday Dell Books for Young Readers
a division of
Bantam Doubleday Dell Publishing Group, Inc.
1540 Broadway
New York, New York 10036

Visit us on the Web! www.bdd.com

**Educators and librarians, visit the BDD Teacher's
Resource Center at www.bdd.com/teachers**

ISBN: 0-440-41463-6

Reprinted by arrangement with Delacorte Press

Printed in the United States of America

August 1998

20 19 18 17 16 15 14 13 12 11

CWO

The
Schernoff
Discoveries

1. On Discovering the Benefits of Electricity

What is it anyway?

—HAROLD ON SEX

It's wrong to say that Harold and I were best friends.

We were each other's *only* friend.

The truth is that we were both geeks, easily the most unpopular boys in the entire demographic area encompassing Washington Junior High School to include (and Harold did all the calculations) the towns of Hillard and Peat, Minnesota, and the surrounding rural area in a twelve-mile radius. (Harold would have liked me to convert all the figures to metric but I choose to leave that to the reader.)

It's not true that even dogs didn't like us, though Harold said so many times. I've had several dogs that didn't bite me with any regularity. However, it was possible for us to be completely lonely and totally ignored in a crowd.

I was isolated because of my looks and my family's social standing, or lack thereof. I was skinny and nerdy-looking until the army started to fill me out. My family was best described as a disaster area. If there was a type of alcoholic beverage my parents didn't consume I never saw it, and the consequence of this was that I was placed well over to the wrong side of the tracks into the undesirable areas where lived such notables as Dick Chimmer, who, it was said, ate small animals alive and once won a bet that involved a tire pump and dropping his pants . . . well, never mind.

Harold suffered from being curious, from wanting to know all things, mixed with an apparent desire to look like a thirty-year-old accountant. Though we were fourteen, Harold wore a tight suit coat with a tie and combed his hair straight back with thick wads of hair grease and had enough ballpoints in his shirt pocket to supply an entire classroom and glasses so thick that when he turned to look straight at you it seemed that his eyes exploded ... well, it was not a good look for Harold and it most definitely set him apart.

On no other level were we alike, but the fact that we were outcasts meant that we gravitated toward each other like two marbles rolling toward the center of a bowl—bouncing apart now and again but generally getting closer and closer until we were friends.

I don't know what Harold derived from the friendship unless it was a sense of the outdoors. I spent a large part of my life outside of things—outside of home, outside of school—and so knew a little of the outdoors. Harold was a neophyte there but he was game and almost always tried to do what I was doing, and I like to think that he learned *something* from it.

What I gained from Harold was help with schoolwork—I broke local records for flunking and might be the only boy who ever flunked shop—and somebody to talk with about Julie Hansen.

Julie Hansen was a few months older and was mature for her age, head of the junior cheerleader squad, destined to be Miss Peat and so beautiful she made my tongue stick to the roof of my mouth. She was completely, totally ignorant that we walked the planet. Consequently we loved her, Harold and I, and suffered from continually broken hearts. It helped to talk about it, and if that were all I had taken from Harold, it would have been enough.

But because of our proximity I was made privy to the discoveries of Harold Schernoff.

I was, for instance, present when Harold personally discovered a new use for electricity.

Electricity had of course been around for a long time before Harold discovered it. Franklin did the kite, and Edison the bulb, and countless others added their inventions and improvements to bring it up to its present state as a functioning technology.

But Harold found an even newer use for it one afternoon in Mrs. Johnson's science class.

Actually, had I been thinking, I could have seen it coming. The day before, we had learned about electrons and how they traveled through wires. On the way home we had stopped outside the school in some bushes as I avoided Dick Chimmer, who had said something about tying me in a square knot.

Harold had said, "They're alive."

"Who?" I asked. "Oh, you mean Chimmer. I'm not sure he's human but I know he's alive. . . ."

"No. Electrons. They're alive. They're in everything, in all the atoms that make us up, so they must be alive."

I tried to get a mental picture but nothing came, just a diagram that Mrs. Johnson had put on the board with little spheres orbiting in circles.

"I mean think of it," he said, pushing his glasses back up his long nose. "If we're alive, then they're alive in us, whirling and spinning. We have the power of the atom in us, the power of the electron."

"Uhhh . . . all right. So we have electrons in us and they're alive. So what?"

"Right *inside* us, all that power—if we just had a way to harness it."

"Harness it?"

"Don't you see? Mrs. Johnson said atoms and electrons are the power of the sun. If we could tap into it . . . think of it!"

And I tried, but I was too limited. When Chimmer was gone and we were walking home, I might as well have been alone. He was already working on a way to do it, making calculations and formulas in his head.

It happened the next day in Mrs. Johnson's class. Harold had acted strange walking to school, not talking much. Usually he was animated, talking with a lowered voice (you half expected him to start smoking a pipe) and pointing when he wished to illustrate something important. ("It would be physically impossible for Chimmer to break you *exactly* in half with his bare hands—the tensile strength of the center of the human body is far too strong to allow it. Though the attempt would probably be painful.")

Gym had been the usual disaster. Wankle, the gym teacher–football coach–Nazi beast (as Harold called him), made me try to climb the rope, which I couldn't. I hung in the middle like a sick bat while Wankle made Harold run laps, which he couldn't, until his sinuses blew and his nose ran down onto his T-shirt.

After gym we went to Mrs. Johnson's class, and had I been prepared I could have watched more closely, but I know what time it happened—2:23—because the clock stopped.

At that instant Mrs. Johnson turned her back on the room to write something on the board and there was an enormous cracking, buzzing sound, the whole room flashed in a white light—like a hundred flashbulbs going off—and the pungent smells of ozone and burned flesh and hair filled the room.

I turned and saw Harold sitting straight up, his glasses fogged so you could barely see his eyes opened wide, every hair on his head standing straight out and his mouth in a frozen smile that went from ear to ear. The entire left side of his head was covered in some dark blue fluid.

"Harold," I whispered. "Are you all right?"

There was no answer. Later I was to find out what he had done, that he had calculated that a dead short would provide almost infinite power to his personal electrons. He'd taken the metal cartridge of a ballpoint pen and a large paper clip he'd swiped from Mrs. Johnson's desk on the way in and twisted them together. He'd wet his fingers with his mouth—an insane touch, that—waited until Mrs. Johnson turned her back on the room, and jammed the pen and paper clip, twisted together, into the outlet next to his desk.

They said lights in the whole school dimmed and that they read a fluctuation in the power station in Fargo, North Dakota, but I don't know if it's true.

I do know it blew ink all over the side of Harold's head and that the school nurse, who came and took him to lie down for a bit—another benefit of the experiment—said he was lucky it didn't kill him.

But he didn't care. Later, while we were walking home and he was trying to comb his hair back down, he was still smiling. His half-inked head made him look goofy.

"Don't you know how dangerous it is to stick something into a socket?" I said. "I can't believe you're still alive!"

He walked on, smiling.

"I understand the experiment," I said, "or I think I do. You had to do it, right? But why the smile when I looked back, and why are you grinning like that?"

"It was incredible," he said, the grin widening. "I was looking at Julie Hansen at the exact moment that I made contact and my electrons fused with the electrons of the power station. It gave me X-ray vision. I saw through her clothes."

I stopped. "You really saw Julie Hansen naked?"

"Well, it was just from the back and I only got through the outer layers. I think I need more

8

power. . . ." He paused for a moment, thinking. "I wonder what would happen if I got better contact? Say if I stuck my tongue in a light socket . . ."

I turned and started walking again.

2. Brain over Brawn

There is always a solution. For everything. Always. Sometimes it isn't pretty and takes a little longer, but there is still a solution.

— SCHERNOFF ON PROBLEMS

"Very well."

"Very well what?" We were walking down the street headed home from school, having dodged Chimmer, walked past Julie Hansen's house without seeing her, and stopped at Overholt's grocery, where we bought two ice-pop push-ups, mine green, Harold's yellow. Since we had not been talking about anything, but working on the push-ups, I didn't have a clue as to what he meant.

"I am talking about problem solving. I meant

very well, we have taken care of the last most pressing problem, and now we shall move on to the next."

"I don't know what you mean."

"What was our biggest problem last week?"

That was easy. "The football team."

"*Exactly*. And didn't we solve it?"

"Actually I think it's too soon to know. Seven had to go to the doctor and the rest of them are still too busy sitting to know for certain."

"Just the same, you'll see the problem is solved. You'll see. . . ."

It had all been perfect Schernoff—turning a disaster into a solution. Harold had come up to me one morning before semester break. His eyes flashed wide behind his glasses the way they did when he had an idea, which was most of the time, and he said, "I know how we can meet girls."

"Meeting them isn't the hard part," I said. "It's keeping them around long enough to talk to them. They practically run from us."

"*Exactly*. We must stay in proximity to them until our charms can become evident to them. That is why we're going to take home economics."

"No." I said it so fast I surprised even myself. "No we're not."

"And why not?"

"Only girls take home ec."

"Exactly. There we shall be, the only two boys locked in a room with all the girls for a whole period. None of the other boys to bother us. It's classic. Simply classic."

And he talked me into it. Not right away, not even that day or the next, but by the third day I was not thinking of the difficulties but of the prospect of being with all those girls for a whole period. Shirley and Julie and Karen and Elaine and Devonne—just reeling their names off broke my resistance. Girls I hadn't dared speak to, girls I hadn't even dared think of, and we'd be with them. . . .

So we did it.

This was in a time long ago when there were some very stupid, very defining social rules about the differences between boys and girls. Girls did not play in what were called boys' sports—baseball, basketball, football, hockey or anything else that required strenuous effort;

women did not get equal pay for equal work (something still not remedied); girls waited for boys to open doors for them; boys took industrial arts (called shop) and made worthless letter openers and napkin holders, and, well . . .

Boys did not take home economics.

As soon as we signed up and went to the first class I knew we were in trouble. The teasing started immediately, and I thought at once of dropping the class. People who didn't even know me, had never noticed me before, stopped me in the hall to tell me I was a candybutt or a sissy and even when I wore a pair of aviator sunglasses some bowler left at the alley, I was recognized and poked fun at. It was equally bad for Harold. We started walking home down back streets and bush-to-bush to avoid being seen.

But we *were* there, and the girls *were* there, and some of them had even started to talk to me and Harold as well and this was so startling and wonderful that we stayed in the class.

I can't say we learned much, or that *I* learned much. I was too busy staring at the girls, listening to the girls, absorbing it all. To come from where I'd been socially—somewhere beneath a one-celled animal—to being immersed in a room full of girls so rapidly was, to say the least, heady and I heard almost nothing the teacher said. This resulted in a largely failing grade and a set of baking-powder biscuits that could have been used for cannonballs.

For Harold, of course, it was different.

"It's simply chemistry," he said one morning while handing me a delicious apple tart that he'd just finished baking. "This whole thing of cooking. You mix ingredients and cause a chemical change. If you have even a rudimentary understanding of organic chemistry cooking is a snap."

"Well, there you go." I shrugged. "I'm a little rusty on organic chemistry."

Before long it seemed our entire life had changed. Girls were actually talking to me—more important, I was talking back to them, something my shyness had kept me from doing before—and Harold was turning out pies and cakes and even whole three-course meals, knew how to do laundry better than a professional (the girls were having him do their ironing) and had become the center of a regular storm of feminine interest. It looked like he'd been right, that taking home economics had been a stroke of genius. I told him as much and was teetering on the edge of actually asking Clarissa Peterson (not Julie Hansen, I wasn't ready for that yet) to go to a movie.

Then the football team discovered us.

Not the whole team. Not at first. But Duane Larsen, who played center and had been hit in the head way too many times, heard that his girl, Betty, was spending time talking to Harold. He decided he should investigate the situation. To Duane, this meant stopping Harold in the hall, picking him up off the floor with his hands around Harold's neck and holding him that way until Harold's face turned blue and he puked all over Duane.

So Betty told Duane he was an unfeeling animal and that Harold was "sensitive" and "caring" and that Duane could just go jump in something cold and wet and slimy and that Harold and I, far from being geeks, were the hits of home economics.

For a brief time I was happy to be included as a hit of anything, even home economics. But Duane told another football player, who told others.

We became, as Harold put it, "toys for the football team."

I think we still would have been all right because we could mostly avoid them since they were always at practice or getting pep-talked to by the coach but it all became too complicated. We had to avoid Chimmer, take the teasing of the rest of the students *and* stay away from the football team, all thirty-three of them, while concentrating on meeting and talking to girls in home economics. . . .

Mistakes were bound to happen and when they did they seemed to grow and feed on each other. I got caught by Duane, who decided to pack me into a trash barrel simply because I knew Harold and could "pass it on." This threw me off guard and later that day Chimmer caught me in the same place and packed me into the same barrel—I was thinking of setting up housekeeping in there—and a few hours after that, when I was telling Harold about it in the hallway by our lockers, the whole team, or so it seemed, caught us unaware. They shoved me in my locker—only slightly cleaner than the trash barrel—and then played catch with Harold, throwing him back and forth like a lanky, bespectacled ball.

They broke his slide rule.

I think until then he could somehow have dealt with it. I know I was perfectly willing to *not* take on the whole team. They could rip your arms off like picking wings off a fly. But that slide rule was Harold's soul, and when he landed on it and it snapped, something snapped in him as well.

Nothing happened at first. A day went by, then another and another. I thought it was all over.

But four days later, as we were going home, Harold stopped suddenly, snapped his fingers and smiled. "I've got it."

"What?"

"How to get back at the team."

"Harold, it's the *football* team. You can't get back at them. They're not like humans. They don't feel pain."

"*Exactly* my point, and why it's taken so long to come up with a solution. I decided we had to escalate."

"Escalate?"

He nodded. "We can't fight them on their ground. I've been doing research. With such a large and brutal enemy we have to use our brains against their brawn. We have to use technology.

We must"—he took a breath—"escalate and use a weapon of mass destruction."

"You mean nuclear?"

"*Exactly.*"

"But . . ." The truth was Harold often dazzled me with his knowledge. He knew things that even adults didn't know. About the mass of light, the speed of sound in water, how to figure the volume of a sphere, how to do fractions in his head. I had no doubt he had enough knowledge to make a nuclear weapon and I, for one, would have been perfectly willing to use it on the football team—especially if we could throw Chimmer somewhere near the center of the blast. "But don't you need, you know, nuclear stuff for that?"

He smiled and nodded. "We certainly do. And I know just where to get it."

"You do? Where?"

"All in good time, my boy—all in good time."

And he wouldn't tell me more. The next day in home economics he showed up with two huge cake pans and spent the whole hour making and baking two enormous chocolate cakes. I was busy with my own project—trying to make macaroni and cheese without melting a pan—and didn't notice Harold until I saw him off in the corner of the room with half the class gathered around watching him.

"What are you doing?" I approached the group and looked over his shoulder.

"Decorating these two cakes," he said. "They're for the team."

"Team?"

"The football team." He gave a tight little smile, about as funny as a cobra. "I thought they might appreciate a little peace offering."

He had used a pastry-decorating device to write on one of the cakes in large precise letters:

GO TIGERS! BEAT WHITE RIVER!

"This," I said, "is your secret weapon?"

He shrugged, smiling at the girls. "I thought we ought to patch things up if we could. There's a big game tonight and they might like a bite of cake before they play."

When he was done two of the girls took the cakes to the locker room by the gym and left them there for the team and we went home, dodging Chimmer and the team, getting teased all the way.

"Nothing's changed," I said. "We're still targets."

"Wait." Harold held his finger up as if testing the wind. "Just wait. It shouldn't take long."

For a full minute I stood there and then it came to me. "Harold, did you put something in the cake?"

He smiled.

I felt a chill up my back. The smile was so flat, so cold-looking. "Poison? Did you put rat poison or something in the cake?"

He shook his head. "Not rat poison. I don't want to kill them. Well, to be *exactly* honest, perhaps I wouldn't mind if some of them died but that wasn't what I did."

"But you *did* put something in the cake?"

He nodded.

"What?"

"Forty-three boxes of chocolate-flavored laxative."

I let that sink in, worked at the math for four or five steps. "That's over a box a person."

"Yes. I had some concern at first. I didn't want to put in too little and have them not be affected and I wasn't sure how much it would take to make it really dramatic."

I had an uncle with problems who used that kind of laxative. He would take one little square and the effect was very dramatic.

"There are twelve doses per box," I said.

He nodded.

"You gave thirty-three football players over . . . let's see . . . over four hundred doses of laxative?"

"Five hundred and sixteen," he said, nodding. "*Exactly*. But the coach will probably eat some as well, which will lessen the dose level slightly."

"Harold, you could kill them!"

He shook his head. "Hardly. There probably won't be a football game tonight, and I imagine they will spend an extreme amount of time in the bathroom and no doubt lose some weight. They may even have a strong aversion to chocolate from now on. But that's only fair." He took a breath and his eyes grew cold and the smile left him. "After all, they broke my slide rule. Did they expect me to do nothing?"

If the team had found out the cake had been the cause and that Harold had done it I expect they would have used us for blocking practice.

But the coach was mental and was convinced that a spy from the White River team—they were "blood-sworn rivals," as he put it, who would do anything to beat the Tigers—had put something in the foot powder in the locker room to make the Tigers forfeit the game, and the players believed him.

Several of the girls had been in on it, but they never told.

3. On Discovering Interpersonal Relationships

It is the complete commingling of every aspect of two people. If it happens right. If not it just makes your stomach hurt.

—HAROLD ON LOVE

"All right, how do I look?"

I studied Harold carefully. This was to be his first date. While it was true that I was hardly the one to judge anybody's social acceptability—I'd never been on a date myself—I had a raft of research to draw upon. I had read every questionable part of every book then available: Mickey Spillane novels, *God's Little Acre* and the most dog-eared parts of D. H. Lawrence's books in the library. Added to this were the stolen moments with magazines in the drugstore, a healthy dose of eavesdropping on the conversations of the popular boys in the locker room and talk I had heard in bars at night while selling newspapers to drunks.

So I was ready to give advice.

But Harold was almost beyond help. For one thing, hair was very important then, and Harold's hair resisted being combed in any direction. Right now he'd gotten it to go in a slight wave back by applying extra-heavy grease. His head shone.

"You look great," I said. "Perfect."

He smiled—a flash of crooked teeth, an explosion of huge eyes in thick glasses—and nodded. "I felt as much. I just needed some secondary verification to prove the equation. Arlene is, after all, quite an achievement for a first attempt."

"Yeah, yeah." Harold had a tendency to talk like the most recent book he was reading. He was studying a book on Madame Curie at the moment and everything was an experiment that needed "secondary verification to prove the equation." And Arlene *was* a nice girl. I would have dated her myself. Actually I would have dated *anybody* myself—if I had somehow had the courage to ask her (I wasn't exactly good at speaking directly to girls yet, not even in the third person) and if she had heard me and had not laughed out loud and if I knew what a date was supposed to be or how one went about conducting one.

I was absolutely flabbergasted that Harold had asked her. He had just stopped by her locker and asked her, right out in the open with me standing next to him wishing the earth would open up and swallow me. I was stunned that she had accepted. Now I was kind of hoping that after the date Harold would tell me what was supposed to happen. Although I couldn't let him know how little *I* knew.

"Listen." I straightened his tie—a bow tie, of course—and tugged his pants down, to at least cover the tops of his socks. "No matter what happens you have to stay cool."

He frowned. "I would find it much easier to do that if I knew exactly what 'cool' meant."

"It's a way to be. You have to *be* cool."

"An example, please."

I thought. "Elvis. Elvis is cool."

"I need a frame of reference. Who is not cool?"

You, I thought, and of course me. Us. We are not cool people. "Pat. Pat Boone. All that 'April Love' stuff is not cool."

"So how do I do it? How do I become cool?"

"It's a way you look," I said. "You have to stand cool and hold your arms cool. Like Elvis. And talk low. You know, like Elvis."

And so we tried, we really tried. He took a pose that he thought made him look like Elvis. But he was thin and wore clothes too short for him, sports jackets from bygone days, white shirts buttoned at the collar. He looked like a large bird with severe posture problems.

"All right. Maybe we'll forget the way you stand. How about lowering your voice—try that."

"Like this?" he croaked.

"So we'll forget the voice too. You'll just have to be yourself."

"Myself?"

"Yeah. You know, just act normal."

And so the disaster began. Because Harold and I had pretty much evolved away from junior-high society, neither of us knew exactly what *normal* meant. My concept was locked into the get-good-grades-have-parents-who-didn't-drink-be-great-in-sports-and-have-hair-that-made-a-perfect-flattop way of normalcy—in short, impossible for me to achieve.

Harold's thoughts on what it was were a mystery to me. I suspected that for him it was somewhere between being the first fourteen-year-old boy to win a Nobel prize by understanding the secrets of the universe, and learning how to dress himself.

At the time Harold merely nodded quietly. I should have known. He was always questioning things, always, and when he became quiet it was never a good sign.

The problem was that the date was still over a week away. This had only been a rehearsal. Had it come sooner things might have been all right, and had it been later perhaps there would have been time for Harold to learn more.

As it happened, there was just enough time for Harold to begin research on the subject, to "gather sufficient data," as he put it, which made him completely dangerous.

He went to the library, of course, and he took out books on etiquette, romance, love and heaven only knew what else. For the next eight days he immersed himself in reading and when the big day finally came I met him in the hall just before the last bell.

"So—are you ready?" I opened my locker door

carefully, a habit I had adopted since Chimmer and some of his friends had learned my combination and taken to putting things in my locker—dead chickens, buckets of water set to tip, a small fifth-grader.

Harold nodded. "I believe I have accumulated adequate data to make the venture a success."

"Good. Just remember . . . well, never mind." I was going to tell him once more to stay cool but realized it wouldn't help.

This was on a Friday night and it coincided with the opening weekend of grouse season. I had purchased a new .410 shotgun with money from selling papers and there wasn't a power in the world that could keep me out of the woods. I hunted all weekend, and on Sunday night after my parents had passed out I made a grouse dinner with a recipe from *Field and Stream* magazine and ate grouse and spit shot half the night.

I was consequently late for school the next morning and did not see Harold until after first period.

"So," I asked, "how did it go?"

"How did what go?"

"The date, of course."

"Oh. Well, to be honest, it did not progress as well as I had anticipated. . . ."

At that moment Arlene passed us in the hall. She took a horrified look at Harold, covered her face with her notebook and hurried by at something close to a dead lope.

I watched her disappear in the distance. "What happened?"

He stared off into space and the bell rang. We had to run to get to class and after that I got the story in snatches, between classes, on the run, whispering at the back of study hall.

"I decided to do research," he explained. "I read books, lots of books, and decided to begin by utilizing the methods of Raleigh."

"Who?"

"Sir Walter Raleigh. He was the standard for dating in Elizabethan England."

"Harold, wasn't that like back in the old days? Like when Shakespeare and those guys were kicking around?"

"Of course. But there are constants. Men haven't changed. Women haven't changed. The equation is still the same—all factors being equal—and Raleigh was supposed to be the best. So I started with him."

We were in study hall. The basketball coach, who doubled as hall sitter, awakened, so I had to turn around. He dozed off again right away and I turned to Harold once more. "How did it go?"

He smiled. "At that stage it seemed to be going quite well. We walked to the theater, since I'm not old enough to drive, and once along the way I removed my coat and threw it over a puddle for her to step on."

"No. Really?"

He nodded. "Yes. And she smiled and stepped on it to cross the puddle and I remember thinking how this was all going to be easier than I'd thought."

"What happened to change it?"

"Well, I looked a bit silly with muddy water all over my jacket and I noted that she stood a bit away from me—well over four meters— while I bought the tickets and some candy. I ordered Dots, two Hersheys, popcorn in a big bucket and two Cokes and all the while she kept her distance, varying between four and six meters."

"Not good," I whispered.

He nodded. "My thoughts *exactly*. So when we took our seats I decided to draw on my research and go to the next level of contact."

"What level was that?"

He looked puzzled. "You know, I'm not certain what it's called. It was a book in the romance section. It had a plain cover and there was no author's name. I thought it was more like a manual. But at one point, before it became more or less medically oriented, it stated that girls like to be touched and they like to have someone blow in their ears and put their tongue there as well and I thought as a way to reestablish closeness . . ."

I tried to digest what he'd said. "Touched? You *touched* Arlene and put your tongue in her *ear*?"

He leaned back for a moment and looked out the window of the study hall at a bird flying by. Then he sighed and shook his head. "Not *exactly*. After we were seated I worked my left arm gradually up around in back of her on the seat so that parts of my sleeve actually came in contact with her back—it was very close to touching. This caused me to lean nearly fifteen degrees to the left and brought me in range of her ear. I turned sideways during a quiet moment in the movie and blew . . ."

I cringed and looked away.

". . . except that the book was not exactly

clear on the velocity at which one should blow. I apparently did it too hard because her hair seemed to puff out when I blew but I was committed to the course of action and I then stuck my tongue—"

"In her *ear*?"

He shook his head. "No. My excessive blowing startled her—she acted as if no one had ever done it before, can you imagine?—and she jerked her head around. My tongue missed her ear and went into her left nostril."

"Wait. You stuck your tongue up her *nose*?"

He nodded. "I'm afraid the date went downhill after that. In fact, she left suddenly and I watched the rest of the film alone. It was a film about creatures from another world but it had no basis in scientific fact. They breathed our air, for one thing. Do you have any idea what the odds are that an alien form of life would actually breathe our air?" He looked away for a moment.

No wonder, I thought, that Arlene had covered her face—and her nose—with the notebook.

"You know," he said, sighing softly, "this dating is really difficult. There are so many random factors—so much can go wrong. I'll have to do a lot more research before I ask Arlene out again."

But I was thinking along different lines. "Where," I asked, "*exactly* in the library did you find this book?"

4. On Discovering Gravity

*Velocity squared times mass equals energy—
except with snow, where everything is apparently doubled.*

—HAROLD ON SNOW SPORTS

"We need to learn to ski," Harold said suddenly
one winter afternoon. We were in study hall—
where we often were when great ideas came to
him. This happened because Harold's schoolwork was so easy for him that he finished it
during regular classes and in my case because I
was so slow I never got it done.

"Why?"

"It's a matter of standing."

"Standing?"

He nodded. Outside a gust of wind blew snow

around the football field and rattled the study hall windows.

"I've been doing a little research," he said.

"Oh." This, I had found, was *always* dangerous. When he entered the research phase of his ideas, he had already decided to implement them.

"One of the reasons we have so much trouble becoming popular and remaining popular is our lack of social standing."

There was so much wrong with this statement that I turned in my seat and stared at him. I had long before decided I would never be popular. In fact I had concluded that if I simply survived my adolescence I would be happy.

"Studies done on primitive tribes reveal that if the social standing is improved, the personal popularity of the subject goes up as well."

"Primitive tribes that ski?"

He smiled, a condescending grin aimed at my stupidity. "Of course not. I extrapolated that idea myself. Of all the sports available in the winter, skiing is the most glamorous."

"Glamorous . . ."

"And if we become proficient at skiing, our social standing will rise more precisely because the sport *is* so glamorous."

"It will?"

"*Exactly*. It's as basic as physics. I wonder why I never thought of it before. All we have to do is learn to ski. How hard can it be?"

I could have pointed out lots of things: that we lived in northwestern Minnesota, where the nearest mountain was roughly a thousand miles away, that neither of us owned a pair of skis, that neither of us was athletic, that I was sure I would somehow be injured or damaged or punished or all of the above, which seemed to happen every time we tried one of his ideas. But the study hall monitor started watching me then and since it was Mr. Marley, the shop teacher who delighted in thumping students with a birch rod he brought from shop (this was back when teachers could and often *did* discipline you), I remained quiet. By the time I objected it was too late.

"Harold, where did you get the skis?"

"They were in my aunt Margaret's garage, up in the rafters, wrapped in an old rug and covered with a piece of tarp. I noticed them some time back when I was up there doing research on rats. There is an excellent rat population in the garage and several central nests in the loft area. You know, they're quite social."

"Where did your aunt Margaret get the skis?"

"Oh. Her brother was in the ski troops in the army—aren't they perfect?"

For making a bridge, I thought, bending under the weight of the pair I was carrying, plus two enormous ski poles made of bamboo that seemed taller than me. The skis were huge— laminated wood four inches wide, an inch thick and a full eight feet long. On each ski there was a binding made of steel an eighth of an inch thick with a toe cup that wedged the foot in and a coiled spring that clamped back around the heel like a vise. When the foot was in place and the clamp was latched, the skier's foot was per- manently attached to the ski—as strong as putting a screw through your foot, I thought.

We were heading for Black Hill—also known as Old Nut-Buster in memory of a boy named Danny Halverson, who tried the hill on a bicycle in the summer and caught a drainage culvert crotch-first after leaving the bicycle at thirty or forty miles an hour. As Danny said, the speed didn't matter as much as what got crunched.

Winding through town was Crooked River. Most of the country was prairie-flat, but south of town the river cut through a series of bluffs and where three bluffs ran down to the river's edge there were hills. They were not anything like mountains, to be sure, or even foothills.

Along the riverbank the city fathers had put a curved park and two of the bluffs came down to the park in gentle slopes a hundred or so yards long. But one bluff ran parallel to the river. Over millions of years the river flooding every spring had cut and rounded and scooped this bluff until the fall was much steeper than the rest. Old Nut-Buster. A two-hundred-yard drop to what seemed certain death.

"It's *vertical*," I said as we came to the top.

"Nonsense. I studied the topographical maps in the courthouse and while the top of the drop is over seventy degrees from the horizontal it decreases at the bottom to a little over forty-five degrees."

Vertical, then forty-five degrees until it flattened out along the bank of the river to run another hundred or so yards to where the bank curved to the right and where if we didn't stop we'd head out across the river. The water was frozen, of course, but it moved fast through this cut and here and there were open holes where ice had not formed. I remembered stories of children and drunks who had fallen through the ice and been swept away, never to be seen again, and more to the point, never to be seen by Julie Hansen again. "We're going to die."

"Well, of course you don't have to do it."

I had thought of that.

"You can let me go alone."

I had thought of that as well.

"And I admit there is probably some risk and I may fail."

And that too had entered my mind. I had pictures of dragging his body home tied to his skis. Better his body than mine.

"But think—what if I succeed and become a great skier? What if that happens and you haven't done it and I become popular and you aren't and Julie Hansen talks to me and not to you?"

He had me there. Julie was the most popular, the most beautiful, the most blond, the most pert, the most white-teeth-with-no-braces, the most bouncy ponytail, the most cheerleader— just the most of all. I on the other hand was a seething ball of hormone-driven insecurity and if there was a chance, one chance in all the chances of the world that I could get Julie Hansen to acknowledge that I even existed . . .

"You go first," I said.

"I considered that," he said. "And at first it seemed the correct thing to do. But there is science afoot here" (he was reading Sherlock Holmes at the time) "and since we both know I am more of a scientist I think it best that you go first so I can make deductions on the basis of your effort, to refine our knowledge."

"I thought you'd suggest that."

"Besides, there's the fact that the one who goes first will earn the most glory."

"Harold," I said, swinging my arm around at the white snowscape surrounding us, "there's nobody here to know if I'm brave or not."

"I will," he said, looking out across the river. "And I'll tell everyone that you went first."

"Oh. Good, then. I was worried about that." And while there was sarcasm in my voice I knew he had—as usual—talked me into it.

I pulled my gloves off and spent an extraordinarily long time bolting the skis to my feet. Then I stood, put my gloves back on, took the poles in hand and focused all my brainpower on stopping time, the way I did if I had to go to the dentist or on one of my many trips to the principal's office. I could just stand here forever, I thought. That would be just fine. . . .

"Well?" Harold looked down the slope. I had been avoiding doing just that, but I now I looked. The world seemed to drop away beneath the tips of my skis.

"I don't know," I started. "It seems more like falling than skiing. You know, like just falling off a building or—"

I'm not going to say Harold pushed me. I don't think he would do that. I was, after all, his only friend and he was my only friend and to say that he pushed me would be wrong.

But one second I wasn't moving and the next second I was sliding slowly, almost imperceptibly, over the edge until I was looking straight down Nut-Buster. Then my skis tipped down, everything hung for part of a second, hung so that I could look sideways at Harold, see into his eyes, see into his soul. And then I was gone.

I was virtually in free fall, with just time to think that nothing human was meant to go this fast with two sticks attached to his feet. My world became a blur and I thought no, this is wrong, I must slow down, and I let out one

41

elongated scream when I curved out at the bottom and roared across the flat park before coming to a stop, miraculously, eight feet from hitting a concrete picnic table.

I turned clumsily, step-over-step-over, until I was facing back up the hill. I wiped my eyes and saw Harold, a small speck standing at the top.

"How was it?" he called.

I found my tongue—I thought I'd swallowed it. "Fine. A great run," I yelled.

"Why did you scream?"

"Excitement," I yelled. I've never been so excited in my life, I thought. I almost wet my pants.

I honestly believed he wouldn't follow. Not after watching me, hearing me. But I was wrong.

I saw him bend over and attach his skis. Then he pulled something from his pocket. It appeared to be a leather flight helmet, which he strapped onto his head. He picked up the poles. He was taller than me but they still seemed to tower over him.

He paused—I thought perhaps to pray—and with something close to grace he slid over the edge. In my heart I sought revenge but I honestly thought he would make it. He was so confident, so cleanly cool about the start that I thought, rats, he's going to do it right.

Then he did something I wouldn't have believed. Just after the most vertical part, when he was moving at something very close to two or three hundred miles an hour (or so it looked), he squatted, lower and lower, as if he were planning to go to the bathroom or just sit down, lower and still lower, until his butt left a snowy rooster tail, a plume of white twenty feet high between the skis.

There was a fraction of a second when he looked like a gnome—a squat shape hurtling down the hill—and then something caught.

I distinctly saw his right ski tip dig in, stop, and go back under him. It stretched his right leg back the full distance of the ski while his left leg was still out front. He stood caught like a great spread-eagled bat wearing a flight helmet before it all disintegrated into a rumbling, thundering, end-over-end rolling explosion that splattered and crashed in a groaning pile on the edge of the river.

The pile did not move.

Lord, I thought, he's dead.

I shuffled over—two ski-steps forward and one sliding back—until I was standing over him.

"Harold?"

The pile moaned.

"Are you all right?"

A long breath, shuddering, then hissing whisper muffled by the snow. "Which way, *exactly*, is up?"

I reached for his shoulder and pulled. "This way—into the light. Come up into the light."

Gradually we sorted out legs, skis (which were still attached to his feet), poles, arms. Finally he turned his face upward.

He had hit so hard that snow had been driven *under* his eyelids so they seemed to bulge. Likewise it had been driven into the opening around the edge of the flight helmet. It filled the helmet around his head and was pummeled and jammed into every conceivable hole or opening so the helmet looked as round as a basketball.

"I can't see you," he said.

I helped him clean his eyes out and he blinked and stared at me.

"Are you all right?" I repeated.

He shook his head. "I can't hear you. . . ."

And so we cleaned his ears and on inspection he found snow packed into his clothing all the

44

way down to his underwear. He had to strip and dump all the snow out and when he was re-dressed and sitting on his skis, shaking while his body reheated, he turned his face up to me and said, "I fail to see how that can *possibly* be glamorous."

"I don't think you're supposed to sit down. Why'd you do that?"

He paused, thinking. "It was all a matter of fear, I believe. The acceleration was radical—I simply had no idea what unprotected speed felt like—and I thought the correct method of slowing my progress was to deploy a drogue of some sort. The only such implement I had avail-able was my rear parts, so I deployed them. Did you—for scientific observational purposes—could you tell *exactly* what happened? I must say I became confused. I saw my ski tips go back under me and then everything was a blur."

"No. I couldn't tell any more than that. Just arms and legs and skis and ski poles and arms and legs and skis and ski poles. Over and over."

"Ahhh . . . Well, that's too bad. That means we don't have enough data."

I could see it coming. "Harold, no . . ."

"There's nothing else for it." He stood—the way a man a hundred years old would stand—

45

and picked up his skis and started back up the hill. "We'll just have to do it over until we get it right. Come on."

Finally, after the longest time, I followed him back up the hill.

5. On Making Friends

Death is easy—it's living that's hard.
> —HAROLD ON CHIMMER

I'm not certain when Chimmer decided to kill me, or even that he consciously made the decision. Harold always said Chimmer was not quite human and was responding to some ancient instinctual need when he beat the crap out of me.

What I know for sure is that somehow, some way, probably back in the third grade, I got on some kind of list in the dim recesses of Chimmer's brain, a kill list or removal list, and I stuck there.

As seemed to happen in such cases, Chimmer

did not develop like the rest of us—or at any rate like me. While I remained spindly-legged, short, skinny and runty well into my first year in the army, Chimmer developed a muscular torso when he was about four. It just kept getting bigger until by the time he was twelve it was rumored that he could fold bottle caps by pinching them between his fingers and had once squeezed a cat with one hand until everything inside the cat came outside the cat.

The thing is, not everything developed evenly with Chimmer. While his body moved into adulthood, his brain—Harold says there isn't one, just a slightly enlarged ganglion at the top of his spine—either didn't develop at all or, if it did, went down the same road as the brains of Attila the Hun, Hitler and maybe Genghis Khan.

I could not remember a time when I was safe.

It seemed that even in my earliest memories I was either running from Chimmer, hiding from Chimmer or recovering from Chimmer. I tried everything—even sending away for the Charles Atlas course of bodybuilding from the ad in the back of a Captain Marvel comic book. If I could get strong, maybe I could turn everything around and spend fifteen or sixteen years beating the mud out of Chimmer for a change.

But I didn't develop as fast as I would have liked—or at all, to be perfectly honest—and the one time that I actually tried to fight back when he jumped me after school he hit me so hard I didn't even fall down but just stood there, stunned, like an ox hit with the butcher's hammer, wondering what in God's name had made me think I could survive such folly.

I have evolved along the lines of small mammals in the time of dinosaurs. Over the years I learned how to hide, learned how not to be wherever Chimmer happened to be. I moved from bush to post, from locker to class, trying to time it so I would miss him or at least pass him when he was otherwise occupied, say when he was stripping the wings off flies or jamming other boys into garbage cans (I wasn't his only prey, just his favorite).

Those times when he caught me were often terrifying and *always* painful.

He had a thing about ears. He'd hold me down and rub-ruffle my ears until the cartilage seemed to break. They'd stick out and be swollen for days. Or he'd knuckle-rub my head until it was all over welts, or blacken both my eyes, or practice what we then called judo chops (karate blows now) on my neck and head. Or he'd lock me in my locker—and could there be *more* shame than having Julie Hansen be the one to let me out? Sometimes he'd just throw me around like a gorilla playing with a tire. (Although, as Harold said, the gorilla would have been much more intelligent.)

By the time I was fourteen I had accepted the fact that he would bully me for the rest of my life, and I'd learned to exist in a kind of fearful discomfort whenever I sensed that he was within a mile or so.

It was Harold who changed this.

As might be guessed, I was from a very poor family and I was continually trying to find work to make money. Harold was from a more settled situation and his parents bought him school clothes and food but for extra things he had to get his own funds.

The world of pinsetting wasn't a place you'd expect Harold to enter, and once he did you wouldn't expect him to survive long.

Next to the Pony Express (they used children because they were so light they wouldn't tire the horses) pinsetting was the worst kind of child labor. It was very dangerous, the hours were very late, the pay was very low. The concept was simple. People bowled by throwing balls down a wooden alley to knock over pins. The ball had to be sent back, the pins picked up and replaced on the spots, and the process repeated. This was before automatic pinsetting machines, and because the pay was so low usually children were hired to set pins.

The scene in front of the bowling alley was one of sport and happiness, beer drinking and camaraderie; in the pits in back of the machines and pins it was something else. There were eight alleys in the Cry of the Loon Bowling Alley and when I first went to work there the entire pinsetting force consisted of four thirteen-year-old boys.

The work was staggering, stultifying. To the rear of where the pins stood was a small pit area—perhaps three feet by five feet with a rubber-matted floor. In back of this pit was a leather-covered cushion to catch the flying ball and pins. Between every two alleys was a slotted ball return groove and above the pin area was a machine that worked with a lever and had a hole for each pin.

Above and slightly to the rear of the pit was a wooden shelf on which the boy setting pins could sit, presumably in safety. The bowler would throw his ball and hit the pins. Then the pinsetter would swing down into the pit, snatch up the ball and return it in the groove, pick up the pins and place them in the hole in the placement machine, and swing back up to the shelf before the bowler threw again.

In practice, it was a dance on the edge of disaster. Since there weren't enough boys it was often necessary to set two alleys at the same time, which gave us no time to rest and required a kind of rhythm that could lead to injury. It was up on the bench as the balls slam into the pins, the pins fly everywhere (including up at the boy), back down into the pit, throw the ball into the return groove, pick up the pins, slam them into the machine, roll out of one pit and into another just after the ball hits, return the ball, pick up the pins, flip them into the machine, swing back to the first pit. In all that chaos it was very easy to forget when the ball was due, easy to step into the pit just as the ball arrived. This was especially bad at night when setting for the leagues. The men were often drunk and threw very hard, so the pins ricocheted and became four-pound wooden missiles, and the setter was tired and simply forgot his timing and wound up bending over just as the ball—sixteen pounds of granite-hard material—came roaring into the pit like a train. It was, as Harold said later when it happened to him, *exactly* like kissing a grenade. Bones were broken, setters sometimes knocked unconscious, and a night without serious bruises and bleeding wounds was unusual.

All for seven cents a line. Figuring two lines an hour on each alley, and setting two alleys if everything was working right, it was possible to make twenty-eight cents an hour, plus tips, which they would sometimes slide down the gutter—a dime, maybe as much as a quarter. The best week I ever had I made twelve dollars and forty cents working every night from six to midnight and both weekends, setting for non-league bowlers.

It was a world Harold didn't understand, even when I tried to tell him about it, and so one day when he stopped me in the hall and asked me if they needed pinsetters, I was more than surprised.

"You want to set pins?"

He shrugged. "I need money and it's the only job available."

"Why do you need money? Aren't your folks able to help you?"

He shook his head. "I need the money for a

new ham radio transmitter. I want to move up to a forty-watt and make a new dipole antenna as well. I need forty-eight dollars and fifty-seven cents and my father doesn't approve of my ham ambitions and since there are no other jobs available . . ."

And that's how it happened.

It was, of course, a complete catastrophe. While I wasn't athletic I had a fair amount of hand-eye coordination. Harold seemed to have a kind of reverse coordination and would frequently—as he might have said—do *exactly* the wrong thing at *exactly* the wrong time.

By the end of his first night of setting pins he'd taken a ball directly in the stomach and two pins in the head, had a nosebleed that had splattered his shirt and left him looking like the survivor of a car wreck, and had picked up a limp. At the end of our shift I watched Harold as the manager handed him a dollar and eight cents.

He looked at the money Ernie put in his hands. He folded the bill neatly, put it in his pocket and staggered down the stairs and out of the bowling alley.

"Are you all right?" I caught up with him. "I mean, you look . . ."

"I am not all right. But I have worked and been paid. If my calculations are correct I need to do this for thirty-six-point-eight more days before I will have enough for the transmitter. A person can do practically anything for a short time if he doesn't think he has to do it for life. I'm looking at it in this manner. If I thought I had to reset bowling pins in a pit for the rest of my life"—he sighed—"I would hold my breath until I died."

It would be nice to be able to say Harold set pins for thirty-six-point-eight more days and bought the transmitter but it would not be *exactly* true because he had been there only four days when Chimmer arrived.

I'd never thought of Chimmer as working. I just assumed that people would give him money to make him stay away—which I would gladly have done if I'd had any money. But one afternoon he came in and Ernie, always desperate for pinsetters, hired him on the spot.

It was something from my worst nightmares. To be working at a difficult and dangerous job where injury was not only possible but probable and then to look up and see Chimmer evilly grinning in the next pit over put me very close to my limits.

But for the first few nights the work was hard enough to keep even Chimmer busy and exhausted. He just took his money and went home like the rest of us.

By the end of the week, though, he was back in form, making my life as close to hell as he could. I'd lean over to pick up pins and he'd slap me in the back of the head, cuff my ear, pour water on my head from the water bottles we brought back to drink from while we worked. Now and then he'd reach over and tip my pins just after I set them. Through all this I worked in a kind of quiet fury. I couldn't think of any solution except to kill him. I don't know how long it would have gone on this way had Harold not intervened. By doing so he solved my whole Chimmer problem.

It had been a long evening and I was a wreck. The leagues were bowling and I was setting pins on the alley reserved for two construction firms. They were pounding back the beers and throwing the balls so wildly the pins flew all over the pit area.

Chimmer was working next to me and Harold was on Chimmer's other side. Chimmer's alley was the funeral-home team. They were very slow and he had lots of time to bedevil me. I worked through it and thought about what Harold had said about doing something for a short time that I didn't have to do for my whole life. But Harold forgot himself.

"Why don't you leave him alone?" he said.

In the roar of the pins crashing and the machines clanking down, Chimmer didn't hear Harold. Besides, he was busy pouring water on my back and could only focus on one thing at a time.

"I said, why don't you leave him alone?"

Unfortunately Harold yelled just when there was a lull in the noise. His words boomed through the pits.

Chimmer swung his big body around, looked at the scrawny, dirt- and sweat- and blood-streaked apparition in front of him and said, "What?" It was as if somebody had tried to stop an earthquake.

"Leave him alone," Harold said. "He's never done anything to you. . . ."

And I must confess that for a moment I was grateful that Harold had Chimmer's attention. I thought, good, I can get to work while he pulls Harold apart. But I knew that I'd have to do whatever I could to help Harold.

Chimmer set a frame and then reached over

into Harold's pit, caught him by the back of his waistband and threw him over into the pins. Harold stood up and Chimmer hit him in the face and broke his glasses. It was more than I could stand. Harold wasn't badly hurt and the glasses could be fixed, but there was something about it all—Harold trying to help me, the way Chimmer had hit Harold without warning, the cruelty and unfairness—and I completely lost control of myself.

I screamed a word I'd read in the Mickey Spillane books. I flew out of my pit and landed on Chimmer's back, driving him forward and down into his pit.

He shrugged me off like a fly. The whole thing would have resulted in my complete self-destruction—I had, after all, attacked him and thus committed a form of suicide—except that fate decided to help me out.

As Chimmer turned I launched a fist at his face. I thought I might as well. I could only die once.

At the precise instant that I started my swing one of the construction workers threw a ball at something close to the speed of light. I heard a thunder of crashing wood as it plowed into the pins. My fist came up and forward and met Chimmer's jaw just as a pin screamed over my shoulder and caught him full on the forehead.

He went down like a stone. The men up front stopped throwing balls for a moment. There was an uncharacteristic silence in the pit. Harold leaned over, holding his broken glasses on his nose, and studied Chimmer.

"I think you killed him."

"No. It wasn't me. A pin caught him. Besides, you couldn't kill Chimmer unless you cut his head off and drove a stake through his heart and even then he wouldn't die for a long time."

"Whatever. He's not breathing."

I looked and at first I thought Harold was right, but then I saw Chimmer's chest rise.

Still, he was stone cold out. Ernie helped us drag Chimmer up onto the bench. This wasn't the first time a setter had been knocked cold; Ernie sprinkled some water in his face and studied him professionally. "He'll have an egg up there but I think he'll be all right. Who's going to set his alley till he comes to?"

I was already setting double but Harold was working only one alley. "I'll take it," Harold volunteered.

Ernie knew better. Harold was still having trouble with just one alley. I nodded. "I'll help him out."

Ernie shrugged and went back up front. He viewed pinsetters as just another part of the bowling machinery, and as long as somebody worked the pits he didn't care.

We went back to work and I was kept so busy I almost didn't have time to worry about what would happen when Chimmer regained consciousness. I assumed it would be bad—figured on him at least maiming me—but the work was so demanding what with my two alleys and taking Harold's extra one every other frame when he got behind that I didn't have a moment to spare on concern.

The lights that shone down over the pins generated a great deal of heat and soon I had taken my shirt off and was swinging alley to alley like a sweaty monkey, stooping to grab balls, throwing them into the return chute, grabbing three pins in each hand, flipping them into the setting rack and swinging into the next alley. Then I came up only to see Chimmer sitting up on the bench holding his forehead.

Well, I thought, it's been a good life.

"How long was I out?" he asked.

I shrugged, waiting for the blow. "Maybe twenty minutes."

"That hurt. Where did you learn to hit like that?"

He hadn't seen the pin. He thought my fist had put him out. "It's something I read at the library."

"About fighting?"

"Yeah. I've been reading up on it. You know, just in case."

He smiled and I realized with a start that I had never really seen him smile before. "Can you teach me to do it?"

I'm not going to say we became friends. If I were to meet Chimmer right now I'd just as soon park a car on him as anything. I don't think Chimmer could ever be nice—there were no such genes in his makeup.

But he did stop beating the pudding out of me and he never picked on Harold again because Harold was my friend. My life changed because of that night.

Harold summed it up as we wheezed home. It was winter and to go from the sweaty, driving labor of the pits into the thirty-below cold of the outside always made us cough and have trouble breathing, especially Harold, who seemed so thin there couldn't be much lung in there.

"I think what we witnessed here tonight proves Darwin's theory of evolution."

We were passing the pool hall below the drugstore and I thought that when I became older and much more cool I would buy a leather jacket and pull my Levi's down to show the crack in my butt and go down there and shoot pool. "What do you mean?"

"Chimmer. Clearly you have started a step in evolution by nearly killing him."

"*I* didn't do anything. A pin came across and clobbered him."

"Still, he thinks you did and that will have the same effect. He'll get older and seek a mate and have young and teach his young not to hit people."

"No. Chimmer isn't that smart. But he might teach his young not to hit people when there are bowling pins around, if he ever figures out it wasn't me but a pin that dropped him."

"*Exactly* my point. That will make the next generation teach *their* young and then the next and so on. In time the Chimmers will become a peaceful species."

"How long?"

"Two, perhaps three million years. Certainly not soon enough to help the world now."

And we walked on. Later I would find that Harold was right, at least in one sense. While I don't think Chimmer evolved, a change certainly began in *me*. I decided then that for the rest of my life I would always look for the bowling pin that would help me through the tough spots.

6. On Angling

A fish doesn't know anything, ever, at all, about anything. Which is why fish are so hard to catch.

—HAROLD ON FISHING WITH WORMS

The truth is I never saw Harold really fail at anything except fishing. All the other times he got close to failure, came around the edge of it, bumped right up into it, but he always came out ahead in some way.

Except when it came to fishing.

It all started one summer night when we were setting pins. Ernie was going to close the bowling alley over the weekend—his slowest time—and sand and varnish the alleys.

"A whole weekend," I said as we left the

64

bowling alley. I had almost four dollars saved and I thought of movies—there was a horror film showing on Saturday night—or maybe buying a stick model of a B-17 bomber that I wanted to make or just spending the whole time at the swimming beach down on Crooked River trying to work up the courage to dive off the high board when none of the girls was looking. Or be really brave and do it when they *were* looking. If they looked. Ever.

"I want," Harold said slowly, "to go fishing."

For a moment it didn't register. "We could go to a movie. . . ."

"No. I wish to go fishing."

"You mean fishing . . . like outside? *You?*"

"Wherever the fish are. That is where I want to go fishing. You are good at this, aren't you?"

"But Harold, you don't—"

"I don't what?"

That stopped me. I was going to say that he didn't do things outside. We had tried skiing and nearly died and as far as I knew he spent the rest of his time indoors working on his ham radio equipment or reading technical bulletins. I couldn't even get him to go swimming in the town swimming area down on Crooked River.

He was no hunter, and the only times we bi-cycled anywhere together were just to get from one building to another. He got sunburned walking across the yard—and that was on a cloudy day.

"I don't what?" he repeated.

"You don't fish."

"*Exactly* why I want to go fishing. To learn. It's the manly thing to do and I want to be more manly."

"Manly?"

"*Exactly*. You will teach me. The way you taught me the art of hunting."

I winced, remembering. He had wanted to hunt. I used a .22 single-shot and let him try the .410 shotgun. We just went into the brush, a small stand where I had seen grouse earlier. Not over ten acres of trees and willows. Harold got lost four times, shot two stumps, a clump of newspaper, and just missed the end of his foot. He finally bagged a grouse so, in his eyes, he was successful. I can still hear his shot whistling over my head.

"But you don't have any gear, anything . . ."

"So what do we need—a hook, some string? How hard can it be? People do it all the time."

"Harold, fishing is . . . is more . . ." I thought

suddenly of early morning light, casting a plug out into lily pads close to the shore of the river for northern pike, of the slashing pull when they struck, of the line hissing through the water; of feeling for suckers and carp with a snap hook below the dam and eating them smoked in iron-wood smoke. "It's just more."

"Then that is what you'll teach me. All about what makes it more."

And because we were friends and he was the only reason I wasn't flunking worse than I was, I decided to take Harold fishing.

I almost changed my mind when I met him in front of his house early the next morning. I'd brought two old spring-steel rods (this was well before fiberglass or carbon rods existed) with thumb-buster casting reels on them, all so ancient I'd bought them for a dollar at a garage sale. I had a small metal tackle box with some hooks, sinkers and bobbers, a couple of silver spoons in case we got to lure casting, a lard can half full of worms and dirt, all tied across my handlebars. I also had a sack with some sand-wiches in it and two candy bars.

Harold came out of his house looking like a

wrinkled page from *Field and Stream* magazine. He was wearing an old felt hat, an older cotton vest covered with pockets and loops, and a wicker creel slung over a shoulder. He had an honest-to-God fly rod in a tubular cloth case.

He was also wearing hip boots, which he had tied to his belt at the top. The whole outfit was at least three sizes too big.

"Harold . . ."

"What?"

But I shook my head. "Nothing. We're going north out of town to a backwater I know about—can you ride your bike like that?"

"Like what?" He threw a leg over his bicycle, held the fly rod case across the handlebars, tipped up the front brim of the felt hat and smiled at me. "Let's go."

It was perhaps two miles to the fishing spot, and he pedaled all the way in those hip boots. I thought I'd have to slow down but he kept up, and when we arrived at the river backwater he hopped off his bike ready to go. "All right, how do we catch fish?"

"We're going to fish with worms."

"Worms." He shook his head. "I read in a magazine that fishing with worms isn't sporting. It's too easy. We're supposed to use lures, flies, plugs and things."

"Those are too hard at first. We'll do worms, then work up to other stuff."

At last he agreed and opened the rod case he was carrying and pulled out an absolute beauty of a split-bamboo rod; handmade, hand-served, hand-varnished and so elegant it took my breath away. I had heard of such rods, read about them in magazines, but I'd never seen one and only knew them as something to dream about, to worship.

"Where'd you get that rod?"

"This old thing? It was in the garage, up in the loft, wrapped in a piece of canvas. I was up there doing research—"

"On rats, I know."

"—on rats and I ran into it. Why—is it a good one?"

"Could I see it?"

He handed me the rod in four sections and I assembled it, oiling the metal ferrules on the side of my nose as I'd read to do in *Field and Stream* so they wouldn't stick, flexing the rod, feeling the perfect balance. It felt alive, a kind of glowing life in my hand.

"Is it good?"

I nodded. "It's good. Very good. Too good for what we're doing. Let's put it away and use mine, all right?"

I finally talked him into putting the rod back in the case and handed him one of the spring-steel junkers. I showed him the basics—how the reel worked, how to lock it and crank it, how to cast (more on this in a bit), how to attach a hook to the leader, then a sinker, then a bobber about five feet from the hook.

"We throw it out," I said, "and watch the bobber. When a fish starts fooling with it the bobber will go up and down."

"That's it? That's all there is to it?"

"Not quite. When you see the bobber go under good and solid, when you know the fish really has the hook in his mouth, you heave back a bit with your arms and set the hook. Use your thumb on the line on the reel to keep pressure and hold the fish back. Don't pull crazy, just enough to set it. Here." I held out the lard bucket. "Put a worm on your hook."

"I am not acquainted with the procedure."

"Oh—like this." I took a worm and threaded it on my hook. "You want it to look good, delicious to the fish. A great glop of good fish food."

He nodded, took about a half pound of worms out of the bucket, and snagged the mess on his hook. "Like this?"

"Close enough—now follow me and do as I do." I led him down to the edge of the water. The river made a large curve there, slowly meandering around a stand of oaks and high rocks, and where it pushed against the bank it had carved out a half-acre backwater. I knew it as a place full of sunfish and bullheads—both easy to catch and good to eat.

"Watch," I said. I snapped the lock off my reel and cast the hook and bobber out about forty feet. The hook dropped in and the bobber skidded to the side and stopped over the top of it. "Like that."

"Looks simple enough." Harold nodded. He stepped to the bank, looped a long arm back and with a mighty heave whipped the end of the rod out in what would have been a perfect cast.

Except that he didn't unlock the reel. The ball of worms couldn't go out more than four feet and then all the energy of the cast went into the rod and whipped the whole mess back into

Harold's mouth, which was slightly open in concentration.

"Yeaaack!"

Luckily the hook didn't set or we would have had a merry time trying to clear his mouth. But he did get a full load of worms in there and spent most of the rest of the day spitting.

He was game, however, and on the next try he unlocked his reel, took another mighty swing and caught *me* in the back of the head. The hook hit bone and bounced out without setting and I used the best words I had learned in the bowling alley.

"Wait a minute," I said when my head stopped feeling like it was on fire. I moved well to the rear, hunkered down in back of a bush with a good-sized oak between us, judged the wind and all the angles and then nodded. "All right—let her rip."

I had explained the principle of backlash to him, but the whole process of controlling the reel with thumb pressure while the line spun out, stopping the spinning just as the hook hit the water, then letting up again—all of that while whipping the rod through the casting arc and aiming at where the bait was to go—all that was way too much for Harold at this stage.

It started well enough. The line whizzed out, the bait flew across the water at a great speed, and then a snarl backlash hit the reel so hard it stopped dead. The line slammed to the end of the tangle, hung for half a heartbeat and then headed back so fast it was impossible to see it move. It screamed past Harold's ear, caught on the end of the rod and described three full circles while it wrapped around his head.

"Yeaaack!" Again he had a mouthful of worms.

I helped him unwind the line and noticed that once more the hook had somehow missed setting in his head. "Harold, are you sure you want to do this?"

He glared at me, nodded shortly and untangled his backlash. I went behind the bush again.

Another wild swing and he cast almost perfectly off to his left, onto the bank. He reeled in, took a slightly different stance and let go again. This time he got it all—aim, release, thumb pressure and timing—perfectly right. The baited hook dropped into the water about twenty feet to the right of mine, the bobber skidded and settled perfectly and he turned and smiled at me.

"See? It's all a matter of fundamentals. You

just apply knowledge to mystery and knowledge will always—"

I'm not sure what he was going to say and later he couldn't remember but it doesn't matter. When he turned, it brought the reel close to the cotton vest he was still wearing (along with the hip boots) and I saw three things with a clarity that is still with me.

First, his bobber *and* mine suddenly disappeared. They did not bob or wiggle, or jerk, or go down and come up—they simply disappeared and I never saw either of them again. Simultaneously my rod, which I had locked and laid on the bank while I went behind the bush, jumped into the water (or that's how it looked) and likewise disappeared.

The third thing was Harold. The reel caught in his vest, the line jerked tight and he flew off the bank. I had used some old commercial fishing line I'd found in the basement of the apartment house I lived in and I believe it was a-hundred-and-twenty-pound test. It was enough to pull Harold off the bank, hip boots and all, and into the water. Something enormous had his line.

"Yaawwp!" He had time for just the one

sound and then he was under. It all happened so fast that I was still standing there, trying to consider that my rod was gone, that something had taken everything when it dawned on me: *Everything* meant Harold as well.

"Harold!" I yelled, and dove off the bank. The dive brought me in contact with the heel of Harold's hip boot, which hit me so hard on the top of the head it made me dizzy.

I grabbed, he grabbed, we had a free-for-all and I finally got his head and mine above the surface. The water was only five feet or so deep in the backwater but Harold felt like he was stuck in the mud.

The hip boots! They were filled with water.

"Kick the boots off!" I yelled, holding him from the rear with one arm around his neck.

"You're . . . choking . . . me."

"Kick the boots off!"

I let him go and he untied and kicked free of one boot, then the other, and we made the shore, where we lay side by side gasping.

"What," Harold said, "was *that*?"

I looked at the vest where the reel had literally ripped loose. Those old rods were made of high-test steel; they would bend but they never broke, not even when they pulled a person into the water.

I'd heard stories of fish like the one that came through. In the old days, they said, sturgeon were huge, so big it took a team of horses to pull them up onto the bank when they were hooked. Hundreds of pounds they weighed, as old as dinosaurs, primitive, ugly, enormous. People said that when they died they didn't come up but lay on the bottom and sank into the mud and just disappeared. I had never seen one. I would never see one, not in my whole life.

"Do you know what it was?"

The reel caught in Harold's vest had dragged him in and if it hadn't torn loose he would have ended up in the river proper, where the depth dropped to fifteen or twenty feet. The boots would have dragged him down and nothing I could have done would have helped. He would be dead now. Dead down in the mud with that . . . that thing. Gone.

"What *was* it?"

But I lay back on the warm bank and closed my eyes and didn't answer, felt the sun dry my body and clothes and thought how much better Harold was alive than he would be dead. He was my friend. I knew that now because of the relief, and I lay in the sun and didn't think of the two rods gone or how big the fish must have been and I didn't answer Harold then or ever; just lay in the sun and felt how good it was to be alive.

7. On the Nature of Wealth

A fool and his golf balls are soon parted.
—HAROLD ON BECOMING RICH

I'm not sure just when we decided to get rich but I have a good idea. I'd spent most of my life working at whatever jobs I could get—selling newspapers to drunks, setting pins in the bowling alley, working on farms in the summer for a dollar a day—so I knew about work. In fact I felt as if I knew way more than I wanted to know about it, and the idea of being wealthy—so I would not have to work sixteen-hour days for a dollar a day and my keep—was beautiful to me.

Harold, on the other hand, had a less strenuous life. He wasn't lazy and was willing to work, but his father had a good job and didn't drink, and Harold had a room and three meals a day, and his parents bought all his clothes. I thought he lived in luxury.

His room was upstairs and had a dormer with a window looking out over the backyard. We were sitting in the dormer, where he had a table that held his transmitter and receiver. It was evening, just after dark, and Harold was trying to talk to somebody in Russia but kept getting a man in New York.

Harold was an amateur radio operator—a ham—and we spent many hours talking in Morse code to people all over the world. Back then code transmission was all we could afford. Or rather Harold talked and I watched and listened, amazed at how it all worked. I could not believe how he could have made the little Heathkit forty-watt transmitter from a kit, soldered wires and vacuum tube sockets and resistors and condensers and coils in a device that would allow us to hear—through whistles and hums and squawks—the little beeps and dit-dahs of people all around the world.

It had so impressed me that I'd made a small oscillator—with Harold's help—that emitted a squeal into a headset when it was keyed. I was trying to learn Morse code so I could become a ham as well, tapping away on an old telegraph key he had given me. I could stumble through the code and get enough letters when somebody transmitted to have an idea of what they were saying.

We "worked" the man in New York that night and he told us about a new car he had just bought—a Cadillac—and how he loves to ride in it. I leaned back, thinking of what it would be like to have enough money to own something like that, not just a car but a big, new luxury car. Harold signed off with the man and turned to me and must have been thinking the same thing because he smiled and said, "Let's get a car."

As with so many things Harold suggested, this thought was so far beyond the scope of possibility that it bordered on the absurd. I shook my head. "We're fourteen and can't legally drive for another year. And then only with a licensed driver after we get our permit. Cars cost money, which we don't have. And who in his right mind would sell a car to two fourteen-year-old kids?"

Harold shrugged. "Technicalities. This is a problem like any other problem. There is *always* a solution." He went to a blackboard he had on his wall near the ham table and wrote a formula.

$$C = T \times E \times M$$

"Where C is car and T is time and E is energy and M is money—it's a fairly simple equation, really."

"And where do we get the money?"

He nodded and wrote another formula.

$$M = T \times E$$

"Where M is money and T is time and E is energy. We simply work for it."

As this happened to be the summer and every able-bodied boy and girl in town was looking for part-time work I could have pointed out that finding work would be next to impossible. But I was afraid he'd just do another formula. Besides, it wouldn't have stopped him. Nothing stopped Harold.

He stood in front of the blackboard, frowning, thinking. He reached forward to write with the chalk, stopped, started and then smiled and turned.

"We'll caddy."

"Caddy?"

"You know, carry golf clubs for players."

"I know what caddying is—I used to do it and—"

"There's a tournament this weekend. My uncle is playing and he told my father he could never get a good caddy. That's it. We'll caddy, they'll pay us, we'll get a car. It's simple."

The thing is, I had tried caddying and they paid only fifty cents for nine holes. Of course you were supposed to get a tip as well, but not everybody tipped. You could do only about eighteen holes a day so you might end up with a dollar for the whole day. I wasn't sure what cars cost but I was pretty sure at a dollar a day it would take us a long time to buy one.

But Harold had a way of saying things so that even when you knew they were impossible it seemed like they could happen. And that's why the next day, Saturday, at six-thirty in the morning I followed Harold as we pedaled the three miles out of town to the golf course for the tournament. And if you had told me it would be the first step in becoming rich I would have laughed in your face.

At first it looked bad. There were dozens of boys there already, waiting to caddy. I bought a bottle of Pepsi for a nickel and a bag of peanuts for another nickel. Then I poured the peanuts in the Pepsi and ate-drank it for breakfast while we waited. Or I should say while *I* waited.

Harold moved away from the rest of us standing around under the trees by the first tee and went over to the driving range, where some early birds were buying little mesh buckets of balls and hitting them out into a meadow to practice. I saw him watch for a time and then he went back to the pro shack and talked to the golf pro for a minute or so before coming back to me.

"The money is in the balls," he said in a whisper, standing close to me.

"What?"

"Balls. The practice balls. He charges a quarter a bucket and he says he's always short of balls. That's where we'll make our money."

He stopped and I waited and when he didn't continue I prompted him. "I don't understand a thing you're saying."

"It's simple. The pro says he'll pay us a dime a ball for every ball we can find to sell him. Listening to my uncle, who is an average golfer, I calculated that every golfer loses at least one ball per round, usually in an area near the golf course named—correctly—the rough. There are no *exact* figures but let's assume that on a given weekend three hundred people play golf. That's three hundred balls lost per weekend and even if we assume a recovery factor on the order of fifty percent—balls found by other golfers, caddies, maintenance people—that means there are still close to a hundred and fifty balls a weekend lost out here." He smiled. "Think of it—thousands of balls lost and we get a dime for every one we find. . . ."

Of course it didn't work that way *exactly*, but it was amazing how close he came.

At first we didn't hunt for balls. After all the other boys had caddy jobs Harold's uncle showed up with a friend and they hired both of us to caddy—at, of course, fifty cents for nine holes.

But our fortunes changed on the sixth hole. This was a two-hundred-yard straight shot across the river, which was about forty yards wide at this point, moving by sluggishly and gray brown.

We watched Harold's uncle put three straight balls into the water, close to the far side but well out into the river, before he got one across. As we started across I heard him swear and say, "That must be thirty balls I've dropped in there this year alone."

Even I knew what that meant and I turned to see Harold smiling and nodding, his mental calculator obviously clicking away: If the average golfer put thirty balls a year in the river, how many golfers would it take to buy a car?

"Harold, where are you?"

"Over here, by the bank, wait—eeeaaah! Something's got me, something's got me!"

"Where *are* you?"

"Oh, never mind. It was a stick poking me about two centimeters below my . . . in a bad place. It's all right. I'm all right now."

I gave up and went back to work. It was close to midnight and we were in the river by the bank where Harold's uncle had dropped those three balls in the water. We would have come to dive for balls in the afternoon, but the golf course had, as Harold put it, "some silly regulation about diving naked on the sixth green."

We were not doing well. The water was about five feet deep and moved around the curve just fast enough to make it difficult to stand. The bottom was hard-packed, fairly dense mud and I had evolved a method that seemed to at least partially work. I would feel around with my toes and when I discovered something that felt round I would swap ends and dive down and grope with my hands. So far I had three balls, four beer bottles and an old driver somebody had thrown away.

Hardly enough to buy a car.

Harold was doing worse. He could swim, just, but everything else was difficult for him. The problem was he knew too much and knowledge can sometimes be a very frightening thing.

"Did you know there are large snapping turtles in this river?" he had asked while we were sitting on the bank undressing in the moonlight. "They can bring their jaws together with over four hundred foot-pounds of compressed energy at the point of bite. Do you have any idea what four hundred foot-pounds of energy would do to my—"

"Turtles don't snap that way, Harold. Only if you attack them—then they bite in self-defense. Don't worry."

"They have a brain the size of a pea," he said. "How do they know *exactly* what constitutes an attack? Maybe my toe touching their nose purely by accident in the dark water would make them think they're being attacked. Maybe I wouldn't have time to apologize."

"Don't *worry*. If you like I'll do all the diving."

Of course that got him. He could no more let me go alone than he could apologize to a snapping turtle. In a bit we slid into the water.

"I think this is where the balls seemed to drop," I said after half an hour, having found only the three balls. "Why aren't we finding more?"

"Eeeaaah! Something just grabbed my—no, never mind, it's another stick. Why do they always seem to poke me *exactly* there?"

"That's enough, Harold. We need to figure out why we aren't finding more balls. Get to figuring, will you?"

This was like waving a red rag in front of a bull and he pulled himself back up on the bank and stood in the moonlight, studying the river. "Hmmm—how fast would you say the current was flowing?"

"I don't know. Maybe a mile an hour. Enough to make standing in one place hard."

"And we're on the inside of the curve here. The water comes along this edge, say at a mile an hour, then swings out there, except that it has to come back into the bank after the curve—aha!"

"What?"

He pointed to my left as I faced him. "There, around the side of the bend slightly. Look for a shallow depression or a downslope right where that little curl in the current is happening."

"What curl?"

"There—see it ripple? That's a vortex. Right there, look right *there*. . . ."

I moved to where he pointed and felt the bottom suddenly drop away until the water was to my chin, and my nose and my head went under and just there, as I went beneath the surface, my feet came into contact with several round-feeling objects.

I pushed up, took a deep breath, flipped over and dove. As soon as my hands hit the bottom I felt them.

Dozens, hundreds of them. There was a shallow hole perhaps six feet across and it was absolutely filled with golf balls. Wherever I spread my hands I felt them. I grabbed and came up with four in each hand.

"We hit it! You're right—they're all over the place. Hand me the bag, quick."

We had found an old potato sack in back of the clubhouse and Harold sat down on the bank and held it out over the water. I dumped the balls into the sack and dove again.

And again and again—over and over, and each time I filled my hands until, after an hour, I couldn't find any more balls even by groping in the mud and looking for other holes.

I came up onto the bank. My body was so chilled I couldn't stop shaking and my hands looked like prunes but there was a hefty pile of balls in the sack.

"How many?" I stood shivering, my arms crossed in front of me. "How many balls?"

"Enough, I think, for a car."

"You're kidding."

"An old car." He smiled in the moonlight.

"How many?"

"A very rough estimate, mind you—you were throwing them in the sack at a great rate so I can't be sure—"

"How *many*?"

"I came up with five hundred and eighty. But I was being careful. I would think well over six hundred."

"Lord." Not swearing. A prayer. A dime a ball. Like finding gold.

"Over sixty dollars." He knew what I was thinking. "A goodly sum."

"Oh, it's more than that. It's . . . it's like a fortune."

At that time a grown man worked an entire week in a factory for only forty dollars. A visit to the doctor's office was only five dollars. A hamburger was fifteen cents. Ten cents to go to a movie, another nickel for a Coke and ten cents more for popcorn. Rides at the fair were a dime. I set a whole line at the bowling alley for only seven cents. Sixty-plus dollars might as well have been a million. It represented two *months* of me working sixteen hours a day on a farm, falling dead into bed at night, up before dawn to milk and then work in the fields again.

"I never . . . never thought I'd see this much money at one time. . . ."

"It's not money yet."

"Still, thirty dollars each for a couple hours work. Harold . . ."

"No. Sixty dollars for a car. We're going to buy a car. That was our goal and we'll stick to it."

I wanted to argue, wanted to explain how many Pepsis and peanuts, how many movies, how many hamburgers and malts it would buy, but he was so positive, so *sure*. . . .

We dressed and started lugging the sack back to the clubhouse, where we slept in the entryway of the pro shack. He'd told his parents we would be camping and mine didn't know if I was home or gone half the time.

The golf pro came at eight o'clock the next morning and he didn't want to pay us. When he'd spoken to Harold he'd thought a couple of kids, eight or ten balls. Not six hundred and seventy-two balls (we counted them in the daylight).

He hemmed and hawed and worked around and fought it but finally he came up with the money and we left with sixty-seven dollars and twenty cents. Three twenty-dollar bills, one five, two ones and two dimes, which Harold jammed into his pocket.

"Now," Harold said as we pedaled back to town, "to find the right vehicle."

Gleaming black caught the sun between the dents and rust, flashed it back in our eyes in a deep, dark kind of glory. She sat there, tires nearly bald, windows cracked and sun-faded, the cloth-upholstered seats worn bare and im-pregnated with dust, the steering wheel cracked and chipped, the spare tire flat on its rear mount, the floor covered with squirrel droppings and mouse nests, the body leaning on her tired leaf springs—she was, in short, the most beautiful thing I had ever seen. And she was about to be ours—or so I hoped. Prayed.

A 1934 Dodge sedan.

"All four doors latch," the old farmer who was selling her said, spitting a stream of tobacco juice that almost but didn't quite miss his right foot. "Ain't she a pisser?"

There had been an ad in the paper for the car. Since the farmer lived only a mile out of town we had left the bikes and walked—thinking we would drive home. We had said it that way as we walked, casually, as though we had a lot of experience, as though we had been at this business of buying cars for years: "We'll just drive her home. . . ."

I put my hand on the fender. It seemed warm, alive. "I think this is the one. This is the one we want," I said to Harold in a soft voice. I was in love.

But Harold had read an article in *Popular Mechanics* about car dealing and knew more than I did. He shook his head. "I don't know. . . ." He turned to the farmer. "How much do you want for it?"

No, I thought, terrified that he would ruin the

chance, would somehow kill the opportunity. No—don't do this.

I needn't have worried. We were dealing with a master. The old man screwed up his face, looked at the car, at us, and smiled. "I was looking for a hunnert and fifty dollars . . ."

My world came crashing down. We weren't even close—a hundred and fifty dollars. It was ridiculous for us to even consider buying a car for as little as we had. It was a car, for God's sake, a *car*.

". . . but you two sprats look like you would take good care of her. She's been a good car and getting the right home for her is worth more than money. How much do you have?"

Harold shook his head. "It isn't a question of how much we have—"

"Sixty-seven dollars," I blurted. "And twenty cents."

Harold blanched and looked like I'd stuck a knife in him but the farmer smiled at me and spit again. "Well, I think I could maybe let her go for sixty-seven dollars—no less, mind you. This is as far down as I go."

"Fifty." Harold tried but it was no use. I had blown it. The farmer knew he had us and he shook his head.

"Fifty-five."

"Nope. Sixty-seven and I'll throw in a tank of gas and that's my final offer if you want this here Dodge touring automobile."

It was those words that did it for Harold. He told me later that the word *car* didn't affect him but when the old man had said "touring automobile" it seemed to have something in it, some high tone. "I couldn't see that much for a car," he told me. "But for a touring *automobile* . . ."

We turned over the money. The old man went for gas and Harold and I stood looking at each other across the hood of the car.

"I can't drive yet," Harold said. "I know the theory but I lack the practice at motor skills."

I nodded. "I can." I had worked farms and driven tractors and trucks. Not much, but some. "I'll take her at first and you can watch."

Of course the battery was dead. We climbed in and closed the doors and I turned the key and pushed the starter pedal on the floor. There was a soft click and then nothing.

"Back off," the old man said, shaking his head. "We'll have to crank her. No problem, she starts easy."

He reached into the passenger compartment and pulled the choke knob out a bit, wiggled the

94

floor shift to make certain it was in neutral. Then he pulled a crank from the floor in back of the seat.

"Just lean back. Don't touch nothing," he said, inserting the crank.

He jerked and it turned but didn't fire. Another jerk, another turn, nothing, then a frustrated series of high-speed cranks and he spit and spewed such a line of swearing that I think he would have been honored even in the bowling alley pits, where Kenny had the record for using the noun-verb seven times in a nine-word sentence where the two other words were "bowling ball."

Once more, while swearing, the farmer attacked the crank and there was still nothing, except right at the end, just on the last part of the last turn of the crank, when she seemed to give a soft cough, like she was clearing her throat.

"Push the choke in all the way." He hung on the radiator cap, wheezing for breath, his face almost purple. "She'll start now."

But he was wrong. He cranked and cranked and swore so much that he at last started over, combining the words in new patterns, cranking and getting redder and redder and louder and louder, the car whoofing and sputtering a bit more with each crank until finally, as if in pity, it whoof-whoof-whoofed and continued to turn over by itself. Lest she be thought a quitter, as a last effort she back-kicked on the crank so hard it lifted the old man off the ground and threw him to the side in a heap.

He stood, swearing, holding his right wrist in his left hand, but he was smiling.

"See? I told you she started easy. There you go—you've got a car."

And if there had been any negative thoughts, any trepidation at how hard she was to start, the feeling left with that phrase.

We had a car.

It's hard to describe what that did for us, to us. I looked at Harold, he looked at me. The motor slam-banged and whuffed over and over, spitting out of a hole in the virtually disintegrated muffler, coughing and wheezing. Vibration filled the interior with dust until we could barely see each other. We smiled and nodded.

Everything had changed. We were free of the silly shackles of voice-changing, pimple-ridden, shyness-tormented youth; we had grown in stature and our own minds with the sound of her engine firing and turning over. That world was gone forever.

We were men now, pure and simple.

"Shall we," Harold said, pointing out of the old man's yard to where the highway beckoned, "go?"

And I nodded and pushed the clutch in, ground the transmission into first, eased the clutch out until she was moving forward, and we left, jerking and bouncing. We accelerated into second—which I shifted into with only a little difficulty—and then, grinding and hacking, I tried to get her into third, but she wouldn't go.

No matter. By this time we were on the section road and headed away from town, the summer breeze coming through Harold's partially opened window. My window would not open but it was of no consequence. I got enough wind from Harold's side and we were moving well now, running a little high in rpm because she wouldn't shift into third. But we were free and clear as we passed the first section road, a mile gone, then another mile, and another, where we actually passed another car.

I pulled out confidently and passed the Chevy

with one elbow propped on the edge of my closed window to appear nonchalant, like I'd been doing it all my life. Another mile.

Harold spit and while he had to rise and spit high to clear his half-open window, it still looked good and I envied him. Could there, I thought, be anything in life to equal this feeling? Well, maybe That—That was a mystery still far removed from us—but short of That, there was nothing like this car and this summer afternoon, moving through a day with the motor missing only a little and the transmission quietly growling.

Another mile and I turned north, thinking I would make a large loop on the section roads and then let Harold drive. Still another mile and I was starting to sing a Hank Williams song when with no warning the engine exploded.

It was not a small noise, not a diminutive sniffle of a problem, but a full-throated, tooth-rattling bang that shook the car, slammed it to the side, blew a cloud of smoke and ancient dirt and grease into the air and shot a jet of flame back into the passenger compartment with us.

"Out!" I just had time to yell. I pulled the wheel to the right and brought her to a stop in a shallow ditch. We piled out and ran up onto the road and stood there while she burned, completely and totally, until nothing was left but the twisted carcass, black and tortured and dead, smoke curling into the Minnesota summer afternoon.

I cried some. Not a lot, but some, a short sniffle or two. "She was a good car," I said, and meant it, and would always mean it. In all my life I would never have a car to equal her.

"She was our car," Harold said, wiping his eyes with the back of his hand. "She was a good car and she was *our* car. How far did we go?"

I looked away, unable to bear the grief. It was easy to figure. Each section road was a mile long. "If you figure in leaving the driveway and all, we came just eight miles."

Harold looked back down the road in the direction we'd come from and then he looked at me and so help me God he smiled—wide and open, his teeth white against his smoke-stained face.

"Yes," he said, "but *what* an eight miles!"

And we started the long walk back to town, into our lives and all that would come to us.

Afterword

Time moves faster all the time, especially with age, and while Harold and the rest of them seem still young in my mind they are not; they have gone on to larger and fuller lives.

Julie Hansen became a flight attendant, married a pilot, moved to Colorado and, through cosmetic surgery, not having children, and never acknowledging stress, has refused to age. She still looks and acts like a cheerleader.

Chimmer dropped out of school when he was sixteen, rumbled around for a year driving a hot rod and getting in trouble, and then joined the army. He went into straight infantry, loved it (as might be expected, he was the only person I have known who actually *liked* combat), fought in Vietnam and retired as a master sergeant after thirty years. He lives in California with a wife who bosses him and a small, mean dog with a name that cannot be said in public, a dog he's trained to chase children from his yard.

Many others I knew then went on to success, more or less. The captain of the football team has bad knees and sells insurance; there are pictures of him as a teenager in his football uniform all over his plywood-paneled office and he makes a point to mention them to every customer.

Marley, the shop teacher who used a birch rod on children, retired to Arizona, where he secretly nurses the hope that they will allow capital punishment in junior high schools.

Wankle, the football coach, went on to never win the region, conference or state. He retired frustrated and angry to a small house outside Las Vegas, where he lives with a wife who spends a great deal of time shopping for things he doesn't like or want.

As for me, I flunked the ninth grade, took it over, barely made it through high school, joined the army (where I did *not* like infantry), tried a stint at electronic field engineering (as a glorified technician) and then settled into telling stories. I raised dogs, too, remarkable dogs that did not chase children; instead they pulled me on a sled in two Iditarods and completely changed my life in many wonderful ways.

And Harold?

Harold went on to graduate from high school with a 4.0 average (he even mastered gym by using what he termed "a scientific approach" that involved leverage, inertial energy and "mind over body") and received a full academic scholarship to MIT, from which he graduated with honors. He then got a doctorate and now works in pure research involving physics, the mass of light, time curvature and other things that I cannot understand even when he writes to tell me about it in simple terms. Oh yes, he married and has four children, all of whom were reading novels by the time they were three and playing classical piano before they were able to walk, judging by his letters. His wife? He married the fair Arlene of the disastrous first kiss. I have not asked nor has he said how their romance got past that first date but one would guess that he used scientific research to figure out that kissing thing.

FIC
PAU

Paulsen, Gary.

The Schernoff
discoveries

BC# 3006100028732W $11.30

FIC
PAU

Paulsen, Gary.

The Schernoff
discoveries

BC# 3006100028732W $11.30